Ten Little Fingers

Ten Little Fingers

MONICA STUART AND GILL SOPER

with drawings by Juliet Renny

Faber and Faber Ltd London

First published in 1975
by Faber and Faber Limited
3 Queen Square London WC1
Filmset and printed in Great Britain by
BAS Printers Limited, Wallop, Hampshire

ISBN 0 571 10828 8

© *Monica Stuart and Gill Soper*

KEY TO CONTENTS

*   Quick and easy

**   Involving a little more preparation or skill than *

***   Likely to take more than 15 minutes (2 sessions if necessary)

Contents

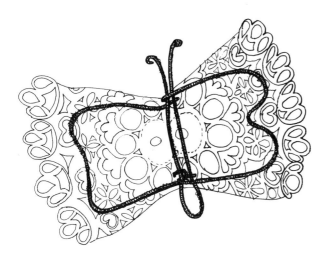

Introduction

This book is for those who enjoy making something out of nothing and who would like to encourage creativity in their children.

As young mothers and leaders of a playgroup we have found that all children, whatever their age and ability, derive satisfaction from creative and artistic activities and enjoy showing the results to their families and friends.

When searching through books for suitable ideas, we found that many of them were too difficult for $2\frac{1}{2}$ to 5 year olds. This book consists of projects made by our own children and those in our playgroup and includes many original ideas.

On the following pages, you will find useful hints on the equipment and materials you may require, but do not hesitate to improvise if you cannot find identical materials. We suggest that you have a large box for your junk materials and a smaller box for your glue, scissors, brushes etc., as delays in preparation may cause your child to lose interest.

We have graded the projects to give some indication of the amount of skill, preparation and time involved and hope that this will provide a useful guide to mothers and playgroup leaders. However, you may decide to simplify or elaborate the projects to suit the time, materials and help available, as well as the age and ability of your child or group. Naturally, all children in this age group will need help when attempting these activities.

We hope that this book will stimulate your own creative ability and that, like us, you will find the possibilities exciting and inexhaustible.

Handy Hints

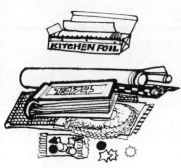

MATERIALS TO BUY OR COLLECT
Paper and Card
White, black and coloured paper.
Wallpaper (rolls and sample books).
Cardboard and thin card.
Corrugated paper and cardboard.
Tissue paper.
Crêpe paper.
Coloured sticky paper (sheets and
    shapes).
Kitchen foil.

Household Materials
Polyfilla.
White candles.
Drinking straws, doilies, paper plates,
    cake cases, lollipop sticks.
Cotton wool.
Felt, materials, braid, buttons etc.
Thread, tape, string etc.
Pasta, rice, lentils etc.
Self-adhesive floor tiles.
Polystyrene ceiling tiles.
Rubber bands, paper clips, pipe cleaners.
Elastic.

Junk
Plastic containers, plastic bottles, lids,
    screw tops etc.
Boxes (all shapes and sizes).
Cardboard tubes (toilet rolls etc.)
Cotton reels.
Catalogues, pictures etc.
Natural materials (dried flowers, leaves,
    shells, cones, sand etc.)
Old stockings and tights.

CUTTING, STICKING AND FIXING
Scissors

Most 3 year olds can manage to use a small
pair of scissors with practice. Choose metal,
round-ended scissors of reasonable quality to
limit awkwardness. Nursing scissors are ideal.

Waterpaste

Wallpaper paste is ideal for sticking paper and
will wash off clothing and hands. We have
used this whenever possible. You can store it
in a squeezy detergent bottle. Put 2 tablespoons of the powder into the container. Fill
with cold water and shake well. It will thicken
in 10–15 minutes. Squeeze some paste into
a plastic beaker when needed.

Alternatively, an ordinary flour and water
mixture works quite well.

Glue

For most other sticking jobs, ordinary children's gum is satisfactory and can be bought
in small containers with spreading nozzles.

Strong Glue

Occasionally stronger glue is needed to stick
substances like plastic or wood. A tube of
clear, rubber-based glue is useful for this
purpose.

Tape

A roll of transparent sticky tape is useful but
brown sticky paper is cheaper and ideal for
most purposes. It can be painted more
successfully than transparent tape.

Stapler

A stapler is a very useful investment. We have often used one in this book but you can generally improvise with glue or sticky tape if you do not have one. A small stapler is inexpensive to buy.

You may also need

Rubber bands, paper clips, string, pins and pipe cleaners to fix things together.

Bostik Blu-Tack (a plasticine-type substance) is clean and non-toxic: ideal for sticking pictures to walls.

Making Holes

Children can make holes in cardboard by poking a pencil through card backed by plasticine.

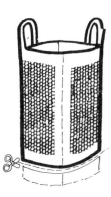

Aprons

Use an old shirt or pyjama top, cutting off collar and cuffs. Hem sleeves and insert elastic. Gather neck to fit child. Bind edge of neck with tape. Wear with opening at the back, fastened with 'Velcro' fastening or the garment's buttons.

To make a waterproof apron, you can improvise by slitting the bottom of a plastic carrier bag. The child puts one arm through each handle. Use clothes pegs to make tucks in the back if necessary.

COLOURING AND MARKING

Powder Paint

Powder paint is ideal for 3–5 year olds. You need only buy primary colours, plus black and white. If you use a lot, store ready-mixed paint in screw-topped jars and put small amounts into plastic beakers when needed. Colours can be mixed at this stage.

Thicken paint with wallpaper paste to help to prevent drips.

When painting toilet roll tubes etc., add extra wallpaper paste to prevent cardboard from becoming 'soggy' and collapsing.

When painting plastic containers or shiny cardboard, add some emulsion paint (about 1 teaspoon for $\frac{1}{2}$ cup mixed powder paint). This helps to prevent the paint from peeling off. Alternatively, use spray paint from an aerosol can.

Brushes

Do not buy fine artist's brushes. Thick paints and thick brushes are needed for 3–5 year olds.

Ideally, provide one brush for each colour.

Crayons

Use the thickest wax crayons for small children. Four or five year olds may get on well with pencil-type crayons.

Felt Pens

A black felt pen is very useful for final details such as animal faces.

1 BIRDS, BUGS AND BEASTIES

Bird

*

Stiff paper, 28 × 15 cm (11 × 6 in)
Thin paper, 23 × 23 cm (9 × 9 in)
Crayons or paints
Thread
Scissors

Quick tip:
You could use tissue paper feathers instead
of crayons or paints (see page 92).

1 Cut bird shape out of stiff
paper. Mark and colour on
both sides.

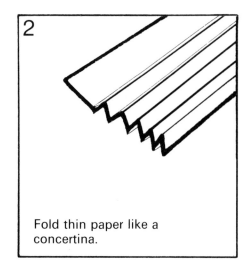

2 Fold thin paper like a
concertina.

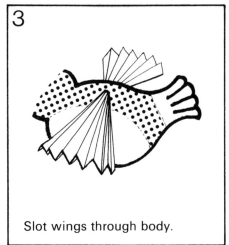

3 Slot wings through body.

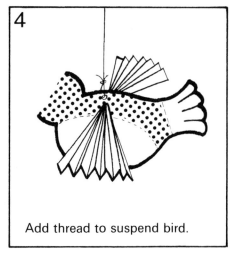

4 Add thread to suspend bird.

Busy Bee

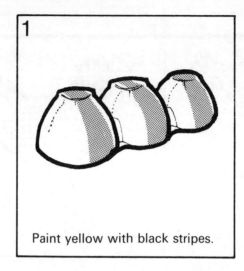

1

Paint yellow with black stripes.

2

Add pipe cleaner feelers.

**

Eggbox (3 sections)
½ pipe cleaner
Card or stiff paper, yellow if possible
Thick paint, yellow and black
Black felt pen
Stapler
Scissors

Quick tips:
Thicken powder paint with paste (page 11).
You could suspend Busy Bee by thread.

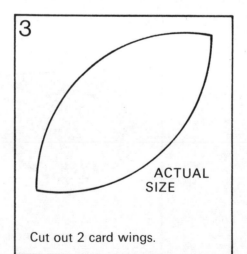

3

ACTUAL
SIZE

Cut out 2 card wings.

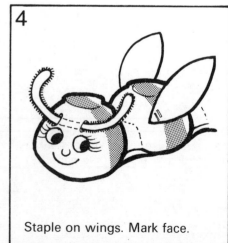

4

Staple on wings. Mark face.

Terry Tortoise and
Cathy Caterpillar

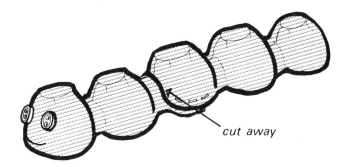

cut away

*

Eggbox (1 section)
Stiff paper or card, 10 × 10 cm (4 × 4 in)
Thick green paint
Black felt pen
Glue
Scissors

1. Cut out tortoise shape from card.
2. Glue eggbox shell to card.
3. Paint, and mark face with pen.

Quick tip:
You could use half a walnut shell instead of
the eggbox section.

*

Eggbox (2 pieces each of 3 sections)
2 buttons
Thick paint, 2 colours
Strong glue
Stapler
Scissors

1. Cut notch from one eggbox section as
   shown so that it overlaps the other
   eggbox. Staple them together.
2. Paint caterpillar.
3. When dry, glue on button eyes.

Minny Mouse

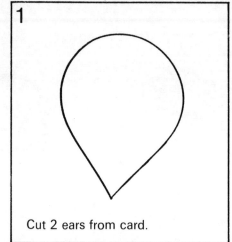

1 Cut 2 ears from card.

2 Paint eggbox. Make slots and add ears.

✱ ✱

Eggbox (2 sections)
Card or stiff paper
Drinking straw
String, 13 cm (5 in)
Thick paint
Black felt pen
Scissors

Quick tips:
Thicken powder paint with paste (page 11).
Find more eggbox animals in this book.

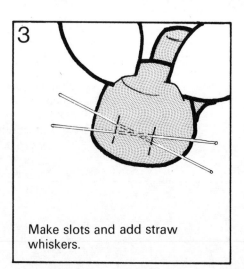
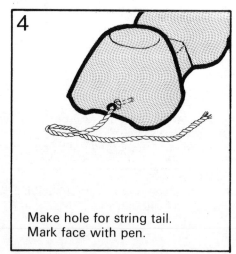

3 Make slots and add straw whiskers.

4 Make hole for string tail. Mark face with pen.

16

Snake

1

Stick strips of sticky paper around cotton reels. Tie string to one reel.

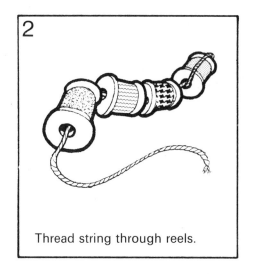

2

Thread string through reels.

*

Cotton reels
String
Sticky paper, several colours
Piece of card (size of 10p)
Black felt pen
Glue
Scissors

Quick tip:
You could use pieces of cardboard tube instead of cotton reels.

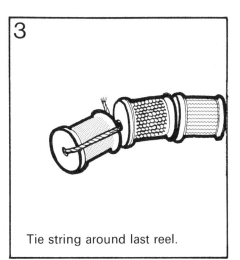

3

Tie string around last reel.

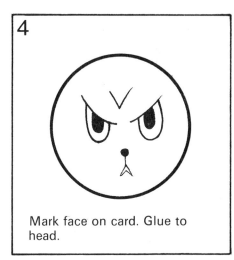

4

Mark face on card. Glue to head.

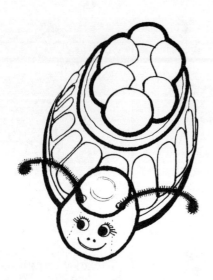

Sammy the Snail

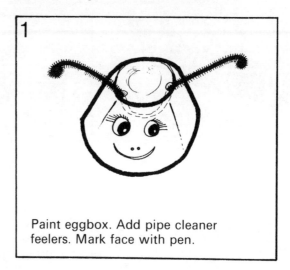

Paint eggbox. Add pipe cleaner feelers. Mark face with pen.

*

Individual plastic dessert container
Eggbox (1 section)
Pipe cleaner
Paint (optional)
Black felt pen
Stapler
Scissors

Quick tips:
You can use drinking straw instead of pipe cleaner.
If you want to paint the plastic container, see hint on page 11.

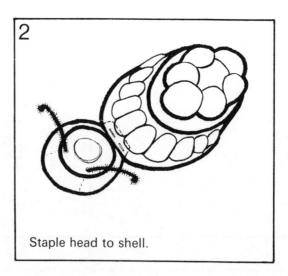

Staple head to shell.

Freddie Frog

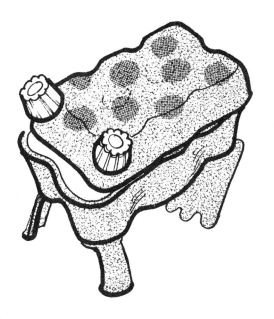

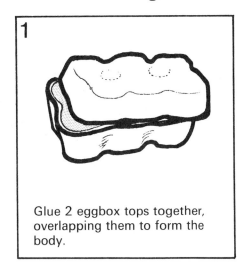

1

Glue 2 eggbox tops together, overlapping them to form the body.

2

Cut 2 front legs from eggbox sections.

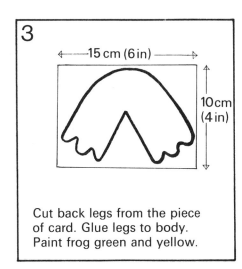

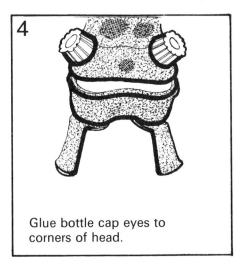

3

←— 15 cm (6 in) —→

10 cm (4 in)

Cut back legs from the piece of card. Glue legs to body. Paint frog green and yellow.

4

Glue bottle cap eyes to corners of head.

* *

2 eggboxes
2 bottle screw caps
Card, 15 × 10 cm (6 × 4 in)
Thick paint, green and yellow
Strong glue
Scissors

Butterfly and Spider

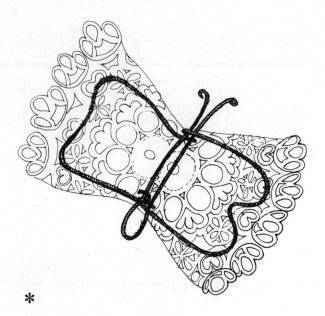

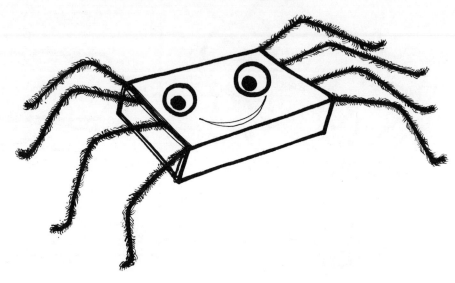

*

3 pipe cleaners
1 doily
Transparent sticky tape
Paint (optional)
Scissors

1. Bend one pipe cleaner to make body
   and feelers. Use the other two pipe
   cleaners to form the wings.
2. Cut wings from doily. Place over frame
   and fix with tape.
3. Paint if you like.

Quick tip:
You can suspend butterfly by thread and
attach several to a mobile (page 68).

*

Empty match box
4 pipe cleaners
Paint
2 round sticky shapes

1. Paint match box.
2. Poke pipe cleaners through top of match
   box and add eyes.

20

2 DOWN ON THE FARM
Chick

*

2 cottonwool balls (yellow)
Small piece of card (black)
Glue
Scissors

Quick tip:
You could make a nest by lining an eggbox
section or other small container with torn
strips of newspaper. The chick could
simply be a ball of cotton wool with eyes
and beak.

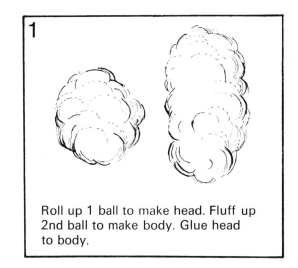

1

Roll up 1 ball to make head. Fluff up
2nd ball to make body. Glue head
to body.

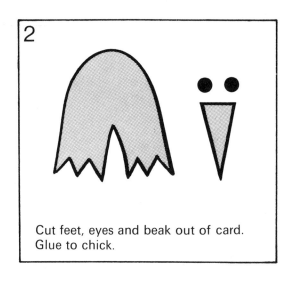

2

Cut feet, eyes and beak out of card.
Glue to chick.

Clara Cow

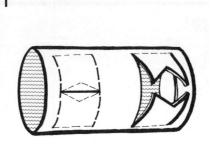

1 Cut the tube as shown to make legs. Paint black and white.

2 Cut head out of card. Mark face. Poke ends of pipe cleaner through forelock to make horns.

3

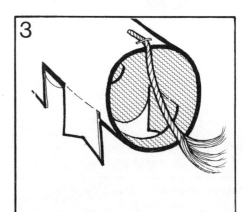

Fray end of string. Staple head and tail to tube.

**

Toilet roll tube
Small piece of white card
Pipe cleaner, 8 cm (3 in)
String, 5 cm (2 in)
Thick paint, black and white
Black felt pen
Stapler
Scissors

Quick tip:
Add this to the farmyard (page 28).

Boris the Bull

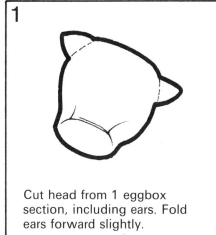

1 Cut head from 1 eggbox section, including ears. Fold ears forward slightly.

2 Cut out 2 eggbox sections for legs.

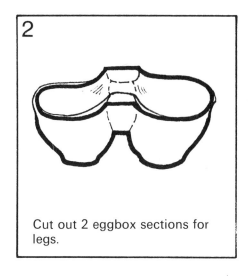

* *

Toilet roll tube
Eggbox
Pipe cleaner [cut off 5 cm (2 in) for tail]
Thick paint
Glue
Black felt pen
Scissors

Quick tip:
You could use a drinking straw for horns and tail or a piece of string (frayed at the end) for the tail.

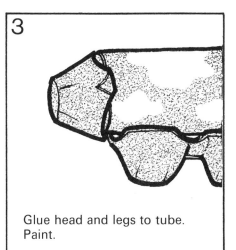

3 Glue head and legs to tube. Paint.

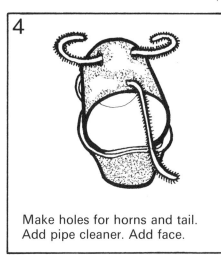

4 Make holes for horns and tail. Add pipe cleaner. Add face.

Percy Pig

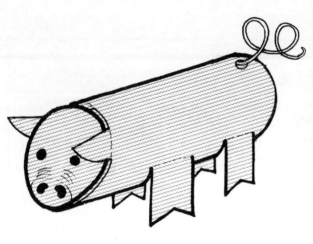

*

Toilet roll tube (see p. 23)
Small piece card (pink if possible)
Pipe cleaner, 8 cm (3 in)
Thick pink paint
Black felt pen
Stapler
Scissors

Quick tips:
Thicken powder paint with paste (page 11).
Add this animal to the farmyard (page 28).

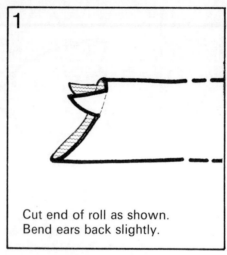

1 Cut end of roll as shown. Bend ears back slightly.

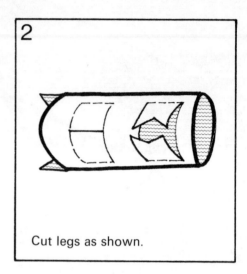

2 Cut legs as shown.

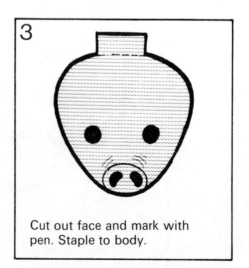

3 Cut out face and mark with pen. Staple to body.

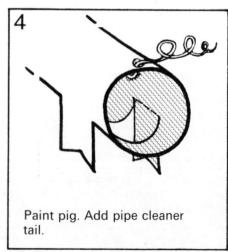

4 Paint pig. Add pipe cleaner tail.

24

Shaggy Sheep

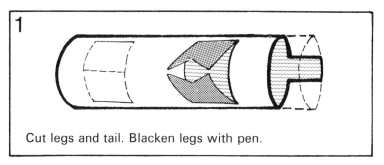

1 Cut legs and tail. Blacken legs with pen.

2 Cut out face. Colour and mark. Glue to tube.

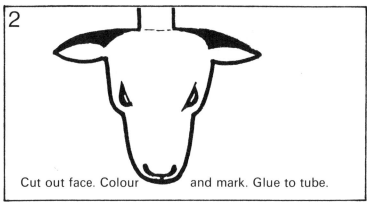

3 Paste body and tail. Add cotton wool.

**

Toilet roll tube
Cotton wool
Card or stiff paper
Grey crayon (or use grey paper)
Black felt pen
Paste and brush
Glue
Scissors

Quick tips:
You could stock a farmyard with animals
from this book (see contents page 7).
'Stretch' the cotton wool over the pasted
body.

*

Cotton reel
Card
Brown crayon
Black felt pen
Glue
Scissors

Quick tip:
Animal pictures from children's books may give you ideas for other cotton reel animals, e.g. lion, cat, elephant.

Freddy Fox

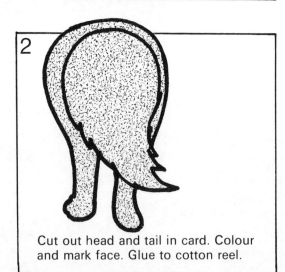

Cut out head and tail in card. Colour and mark face. Glue to cotton reel.

Horace the Horse

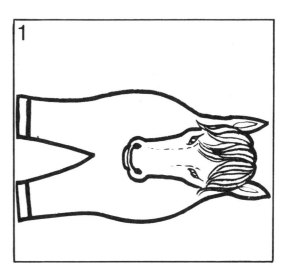

*

Cotton reel
Card
Crayons
Black felt pen
Glue
Scissors

Quick tips:
Your horse could pull a wagon (page 45–6).
You could make a stable out of a box.

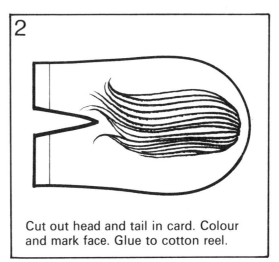

Cut out head and tail in card. Colour
and mark face. Glue to cotton reel.

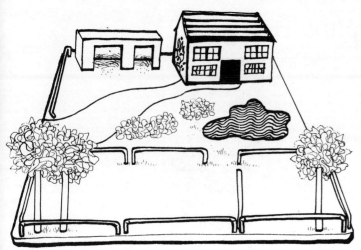

Farmyard

***

Polystyrene ceiling tile, 60 × 60 cm
(24 × 24 in), or several 30 × 30 cm
(12 × 12 in) tiles on cardboard base
Cardboard boxes
Corrugated paper or cardboard
Tissue paper, green
Plastic drinking straws
Matches (used)
Paint, green, brown, blue and red
Black felt pen
Glue
Scissors

Quick tips:
Easily adapted for a group project.
Add the farmyard animals from this chapter.
Make other box buildings—hen-house, pigsty etc.

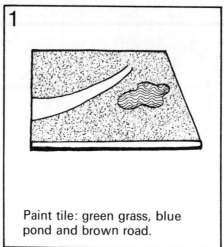

1 Paint tile: green grass, blue pond and brown road.

2 Barn: box cut as shown. Paint.

fold

House: box with corrugated card roof glued on. Paint.

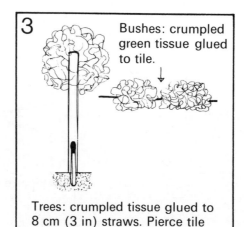

3 Bushes: crumpled green tissue glued to tile.

Trees: crumpled tissue glued to 8 cm (3 in) straws. Pierce tile with match and place tree over it.

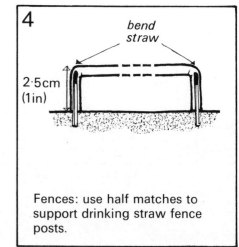

4 *bend straw*

2·5 cm (1 in)

Fences: use half matches to support drinking straw fence posts.

3 ANIMAL MAGIC

Conny Camel

**

2 toilet roll tubes
Eggbox (2 sections)
Small piece of card or stiff paper
8 cm (3 in) string, frayed at one end
4 lollipop sticks
Thick brown paint
Black felt pen
Glue
Stapler
Scissors

Quick tip:
Thicken powder paint with paste (page 11).

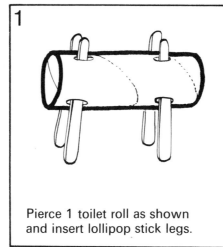

1 Pierce 1 toilet roll as shown and insert lollipop stick legs.

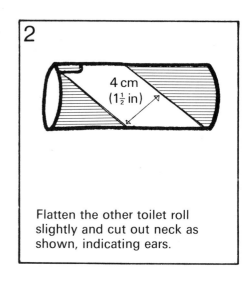

2 Flatten the other toilet roll slightly and cut out neck as shown, indicating ears.

4 cm
(1½ in)

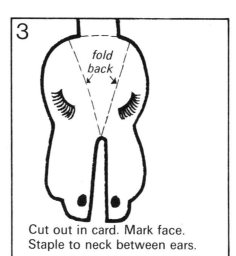

3 *fold back*

Cut out in card. Mark face. Staple to neck between ears.

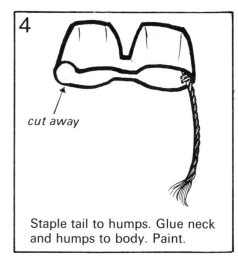

4 *cut away*

Staple tail to humps. Glue neck and humps to body. Paint.

29

Gerry Giraffe

**

Toilet roll tube
Kitchen towel tube
8 cm (3 in) string, frayed at one end
Thick paint, yellow and orange
Black felt pen
Sticky tape
Scissors
Ruler

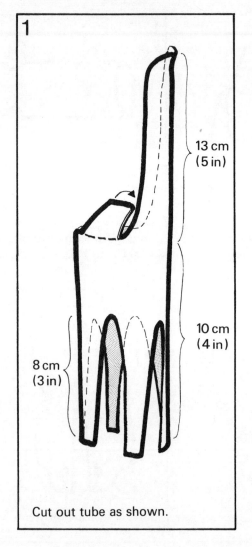

1

13 cm (5 in)

10 cm (4 in)

8 cm (3 in)

Cut out tube as shown.

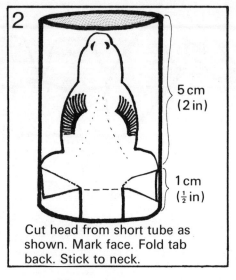

2

5 cm (2 in)

1 cm (½ in)

Cut head from short tube as shown. Mark face. Fold tab back. Stick to neck.

3

Stick tail to back. Fold back over and stick down. Paint.

Lenny the Lion

**

Toilet roll tube
Eggbox (2 sections)
8 cm (3 in) string, frayed at one end
Card or stiff paper, yellow if possible
Thick yellow paint
Black felt pen
Stapler
Scissors

Quick tips:
Find more toilet roll animals in this book.
Thicken powder paint with paste (page 11).

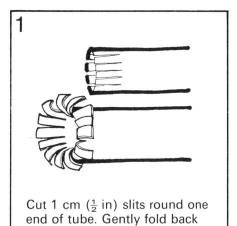

1

Cut 1 cm ($\frac{1}{2}$ in) slits round one end of tube. Gently fold back mane.

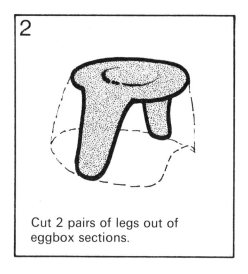

2

Cut 2 pairs of legs out of eggbox sections.

3

Cut face out of card. Paint if necessary. Mark with pen. Fold tab back and ears forward.

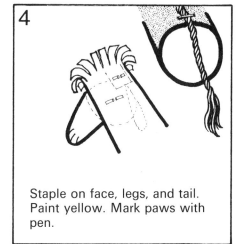

4

Staple on face, legs, and tail. Paint yellow. Mark paws with pen.

Leopard (or Tiger)

** **

Toilet roll tube
Eggbox (2 sections)
8 cm (3 in) string, frayed at one end
Card or stiff paper
Thick paint, yellow and black
Black felt pen
Stapler
Scissors

Quick tips:
Thicken powder paint with paste (page 11).
Make a zoo for your animals (page 37).

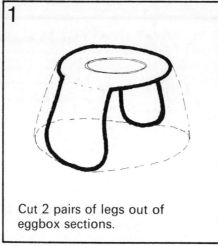

1 Cut 2 pairs of legs out of eggbox sections.

2 Cut face out of card, mark with pen. Fold flap back and ears forward.

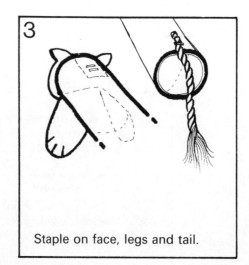

3 Staple on face, legs and tail.

4 Paint yellow with black spots or stripes. Mark paws with pen.

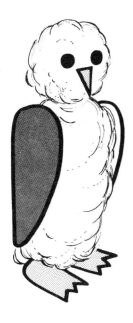

*

2 cotton wool balls
Small piece of black card
Small piece of yellow card
Glue
Scissors

Penguin

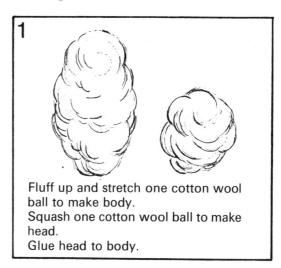

1

Fluff up and stretch one cotton wool ball to make body.
Squash one cotton wool ball to make head.
Glue head to body.

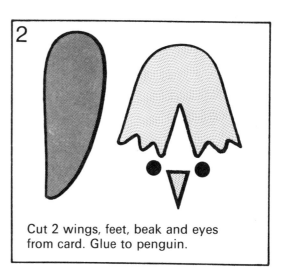

2

Cut 2 wings, feet, beak and eyes from card. Glue to penguin.

Tommy Turtle

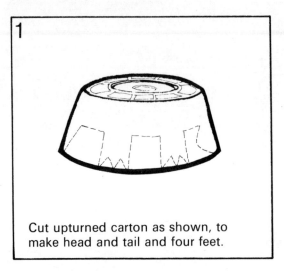

Cut upturned carton as shown, to make head and tail and four feet.

*

Large plastic cottage cheese carton
Thick green paint
Black felt pen
Scissors

Quick tip:
For hint on painting plastic see page 11.

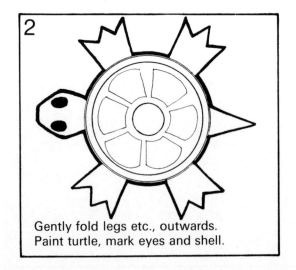

Gently fold legs etc., outwards.
Paint turtle, mark eyes and shell.

Stocking Rabbit and Cat

*

Nylon stocking
Rubber band
Newspaper
Small piece of card
Cotton wool (for rabbit)
3 broom bristles
Black felt pen
Glue
Scissors

Quick tip:
You could make hand puppets by stuffing
the head only and leaving the tail end open.

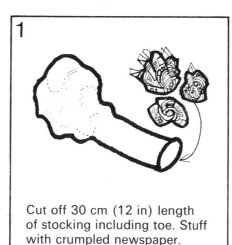

1 Cut off 30 cm (12 in) length
of stocking including toe. Stuff
with crumpled newspaper.

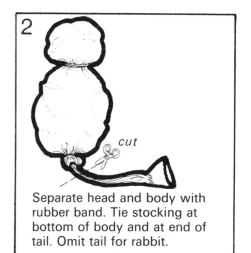

2 Separate head and body with
rubber band. Tie stocking at
bottom of body and at end of
tail. Omit tail for rabbit.

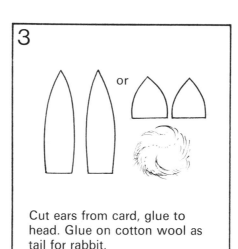

3 Cut ears from card, glue to
head. Glue on cotton wool as
tail for rabbit.

4 Poke bristles through face to
make whiskers. Mark face with
pen.

Exotic Birds and Fishes

*

Toilet roll tubes
Pieces of card
Eggboxes
Doilies . . . etc.
Paints
Glue
Scissors

Quick tip:
You could hang several creatures from a
coat hanger to make a mobile.

Design your own creatures
using these and any other odds
and ends.
You can use your imagination
to make them as exotic and
colourful as possible.

***

Cardboard boxes
Polystyrene tiles
Eggboxes
Plastic drinking straws
Tin foil
Matches
Paint
Glue
Scissors

Quick tips:
Use tissue boxes and gift boxes for cages of different shapes and sizes.
Pipe cleaners or lollipop sticks can be used for cage bars.
Make a frieze of a zoo, using cut-out animal pictures.
Design a Noah's ark to house the animals. You could use boxes or a large plastic detergent container.

Zoo

1 PENGUIN POOL

Cut pool from tin foil. Glue to polystyrene tile. Make rocks with eggbox sections. Paint brown.

2 PADDOCK

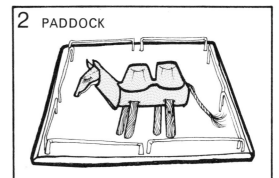

Paint polystyrene tile green. Make match and straw fences, (see farmyard on page 28).

Aeroplane

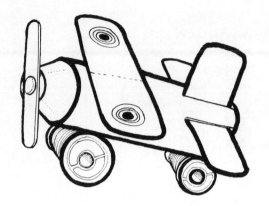

**

Toilet roll tube
Piece of card about 15 × 15 cm
(6 × 6 in)
1 eggbox section
2 cotton reels (one large, one small)
Brass paper clip
Thick paint
Glue
Scissors

Quick tip:
You could make an aerodrome layout on a large piece of cardboard, adding box buildings (see Toytown, page 89), and a control tower, based on the Lighthouse (page 52).

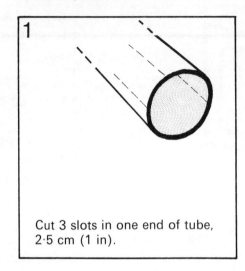

1

Cut 3 slots in one end of tube, 2·5 cm (1 in).

2

10 cm (4 in)

8 cm (3 in)

2·5 cm (1 in)

Cut out 2 pieces of card for the tail. Cut slots half-way through as shown. Slot 2 pieces together. Slot tail into tube.

3

15 cm (6 in)

5 cm (2 in)

Cut piece of card for wings. Glue to tube. Glue cotton reel wheels to tube.

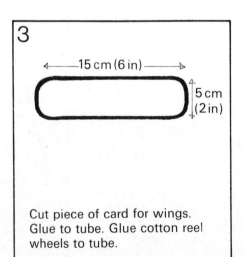

4

8 cm (3 in)

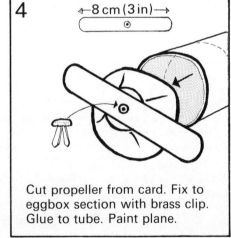

Cut propeller from card. Fix to eggbox section with brass clip. Glue to tube. Paint plane.

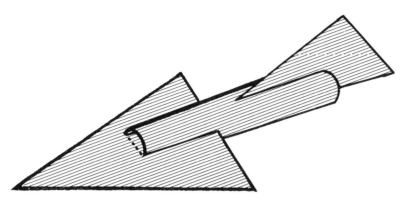

Jet Plane

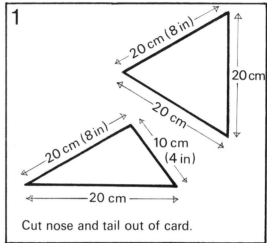

1

20 cm (8 in)
20 cm
20 cm
20 cm (8 in)
20 cm
10 cm (4 in)
20 cm

Cut nose and tail out of card.

*

Kitchen towel tube
2 pieces of card
Thick paint
Scissors

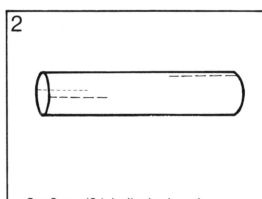

2

Cut 8 cm (3 in) slits in the tube as shown. Slot nose and tail into the tube. Paint.

Rocket (1) and Rocket (2)

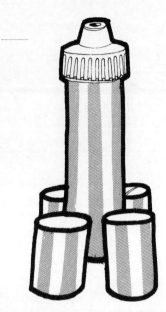

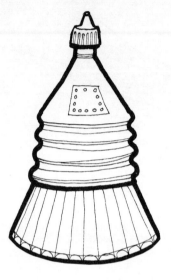

**

Plastic bottle and top
Cottage cheese carton
Small screw cap
Thick paint
Glue
Scissors

**

4 toilet roll tubes cut to 9 cm (3½ in)
Kitchen towel tube
Screw lid
Screw cap
Thick paint
Glue
Stapler

1. Staple or glue toilet rolls to kitchen
   towel tube.
2. Glue lid and cap to tube to form nose
   cone.
3. Paint rocket.

Quick tip:
You can design your own rocket using
cardboard tubes, plastic beakers, tops etc.

1. Cut bottle below neck.
2. Glue bottle to upturned cottage cheese
   carton.
3. Glue cap to screw top of bottle.
4. Paint (see hint on page 11).

Quick tips:
You could make a moonscape by gluing
torn-off eggbox sections, rings of toilet roll
tubes and eggshells to a cardboard base.
Paint grey, white and black and glue tin
foil inside 'craters'.
Design your own spaceman, beginning
with a toilet roll tube covered with tin foil.

Rocket (3)

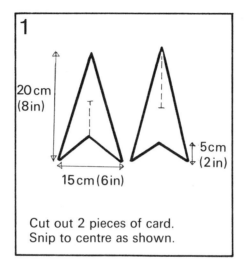

1 Cut out 2 pieces of card. Snip to centre as shown.

20 cm (8 in)
15 cm (6 in)
5 cm (2 in)

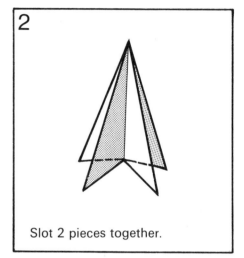

2 Slot 2 pieces together.

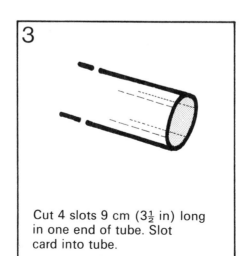

3 Cut 4 slots 9 cm (3½ in) long in one end of tube. Slot card into tube.

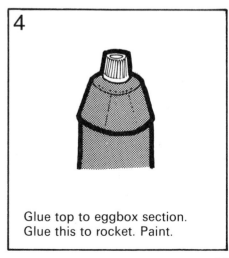

4 Glue top to eggbox section. Glue this to rocket. Paint.

**

Kitchen towel tube
Eggbox (1 section)
Toothpaste tube top
Cardboard, 20 × 30 cm (8 × 12 in)
Thick paint
Glue
Scissors

Roger the Racing Car

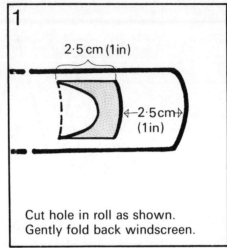

1 Cut hole in roll as shown. Gently fold back windscreen.

2·5 cm (1in)

2·5 cm (1in)

2 Staple other end of tube as shown. Paint. Add stripes and numbers if you like.

*

Toilet roll tube
Card or 4 bottle tops
Glue
Thick paint (1 or 2 colours)
Stapler
Scissors

Quick tips:
You could use strips of coloured sticky paper to make stripes.
Thicken powder paint with paste (page 11).
Make a child-size car from a large box.

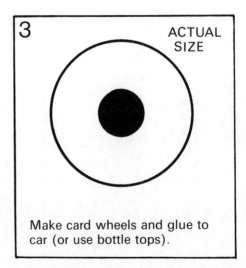

3 ACTUAL SIZE

Make card wheels and glue to car (or use bottle tops).

** **

Toilet roll tube
Large toothpaste box
2 cotton reels
Toothpaste tube top
Small piece of card
2 rubber bands
Thick paint
Black felt pen
Glue
Stapler
Scissors

Quick tips:
You can make holes in cardboard with a
pencil (page 11).
Thicken powder paint with paste (page 11).
The cotton reels could be stuck on with
strong glue.
Make your own trucks out of boxes with
cotton reel wheels.

Eddy Engine

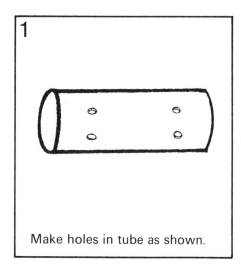

Make holes in tube as shown.

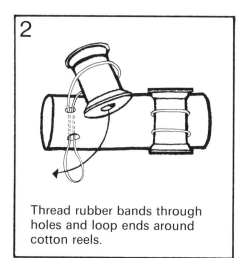

Thread rubber bands through
holes and loop ends around
cotton reels.

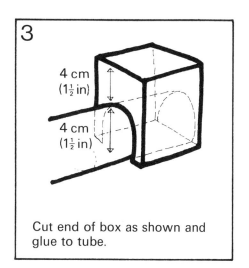

4 cm
(1½ in)

4 cm
(1½ in)

Cut end of box as shown and
glue to tube.

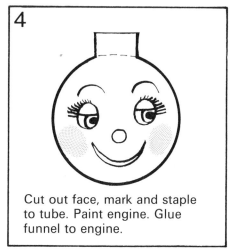

Cut out face, mark and staple
to tube. Paint engine. Glue
funnel to engine.

Steamroller

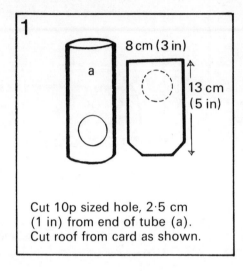

1

8 cm (3 in)

13 cm (5 in)

a

Cut 10p sized hole, 2·5 cm (1 in) from end of tube (a). Cut roof from card as shown.

2

b

c

Fix ½ tube (b) to tube (c) with brass paper clip.

**

Cheese box lid and base
2½ toilet roll tubes
Card, 8 × 13 cm (3 × 5 in)
Toothpaste tube top
3 brass paper clips
Thick paint
Glue
Scissors

Quick tips:
Thicken powder paint with paste (page 11).
You can add a face to your steamroller (see engine page 43).
Very young children may find it easier to paint the steamroller before putting it together.

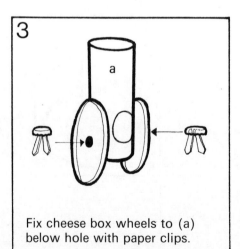

3

a

Fix cheese box wheels to (a) below hole with paper clips.

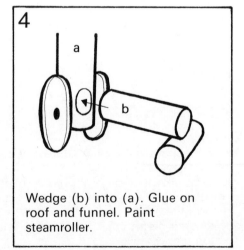

4

a

b

Wedge (b) into (a). Glue on roof and funnel. Paint steamroller.

Wagon (1)

**

Large toothpaste box
Corrugated paper (e.g., from tin of biscuits)
2 lollipop sticks
2 circles of card, 4 cm (1½ in) diameter
Black felt pen
Paint
Glue
Scissors

Quick tip:
Make a horse to pull the wagon (page 27).

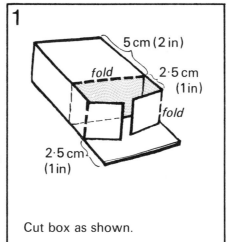

1

5 cm (2 in)

fold

2·5 cm (1 in)

fold

2·5 cm (1 in)

Cut box as shown.

2

8 cm (3 in)

15 cm (6 in)

8 cm (3 in)

2·5 cm (1 in)

Cut paper as shown.

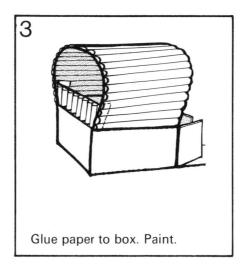

3

Glue paper to box. Paint.

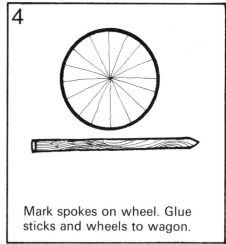

4

Mark spokes on wheel. Glue sticks and wheels to wagon.

Wagon (2)

1

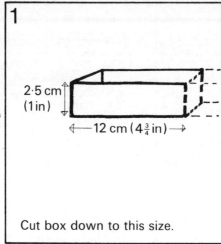

2·5 cm (1 in)

← 12 cm (4¾ in) →

Cut box down to this size.

2

Cut tube down centre. Stretch
open slightly, glue to box.
Paint.

**

Small toothpaste box
Toilet roll tube
4 circles of card, 4 cm (1½ in) diameter
2 pipe cleaners
Thick paint
Black felt pen
Glue
Scissors

Quick tips:
Make a horse to pull your wagon (page 27).
For hint on making holes in cardboard, see
page 11.

3

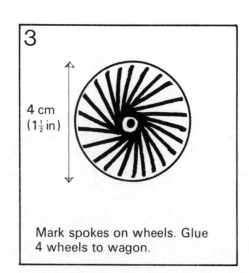

4 cm
(1½ in)

Mark spokes on wheels. Glue
4 wheels to wagon.

4

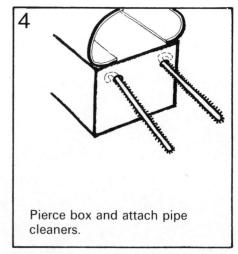

Pierce box and attach pipe
cleaners.

Windmill

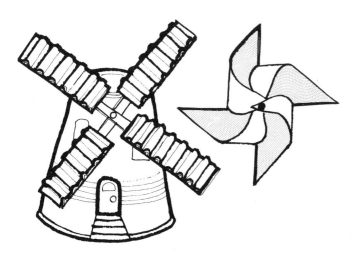

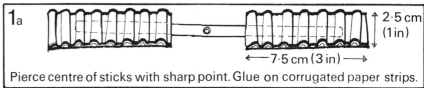

1a 2·5 cm (1 in)

7·5 cm (3 in)

Pierce centre of sticks with sharp point. Glue on corrugated paper strips.

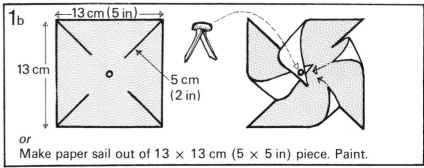

1b ←—13 cm (5 in)—→

13 cm

5 cm (2 in)

or
Make paper sail out of 13 × 13 cm (5 × 5 in) piece. Paint.

2

Paint container. Mark door, etc., with pen. Fix sails with clip.

✳✳

Container such as $\frac{1}{2}$ pint cream carton or
Squeezy bottle (with base cut off)
2 lollipop sticks
Corrugated paper
or stiff coloured paper
   13 × 13 cm (5 × 5 in)
Glue
Brass paper clip
Thick paint
Black felt pen
Scissors

Quick tips:
For hint on painting plastic containers see
page 11.
Make simple cardboard sails if you prefer.

Bus

Large cereal box
2 toilet roll tubes
Small piece of card
Thick red paint
Sticky tape
Glue
Scissors

Quick tips:
Add emulsion paint to powder paint
(page 11).
Design your own vehicles using boxes of
all shapes and sizes.

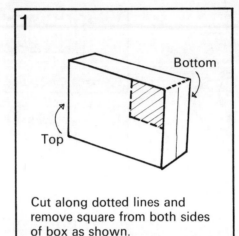

1

Cut along dotted lines and
remove square from both sides
of box as shown.

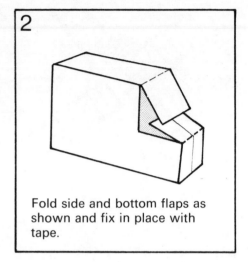

2

Fold side and bottom flaps as
shown and fix in place with
tape.

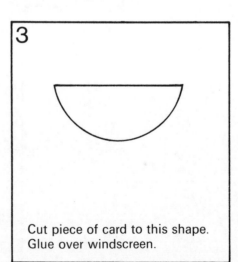

3

Cut piece of card to this shape.
Glue over windscreen.

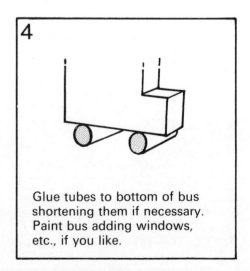

4

Glue tubes to bottom of bus
shortening them if necessary.
Paint bus adding windows,
etc., if you like.

Flat Fish

*

White card or stiff paper,
25 × 30 cm (10 × 12 in)
Bright tissue paper
Wallpaper paste and brush
Thread
Black felt pen or crayon
Scissors

Quick tips:
Cut tissue many layers at a time.
Repeat decoration on the other side of the fish if you like.
See page 92 for more tissue paper ideas.

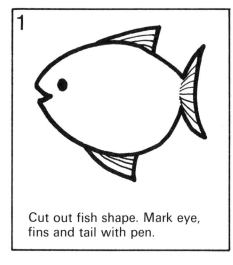

1 Cut out fish shape. Mark eye, fins and tail with pen.

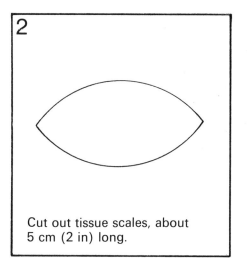

2 Cut out tissue scales, about 5 cm (2 in) long.

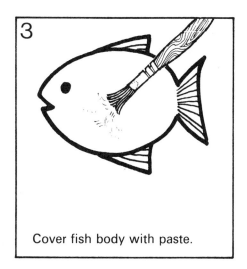

3 Cover fish body with paste.

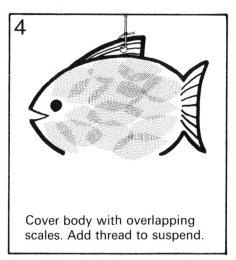

4 Cover body with overlapping scales. Add thread to suspend.

Sail Boats

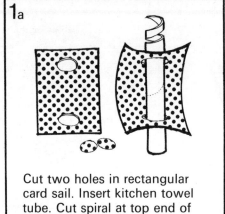

1a

Cut two holes in rectangular card sail. Insert kitchen towel tube. Cut spiral at top end of tube.

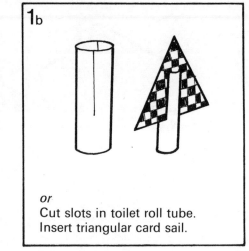

1b

or
Cut slots in toilet roll tube. Insert triangular card sail.

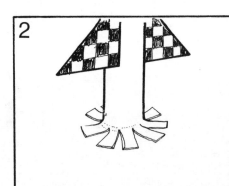

2

Cut bottom of tube. Fold flaps outwards. Glue mast to boat. Paint mast and sail.

Plastic cartons (e.g., margarine)
Cardboard tubes
Card
Thick paint
Glue
Scissors

Quick tips:
Make a seascape for your boats by pasting sand and tissue paper waves to a sheet of paper on a table (see Chapter 10). Add pebbles, shells, etc. and a lighthouse (page 52).

Steamship

**

Margarine carton, oblong if possible
Plastic liquid detergent bottle or similar
Strong glue
Water-proof marking pen
Scissors
Serrated kitchen knife

1

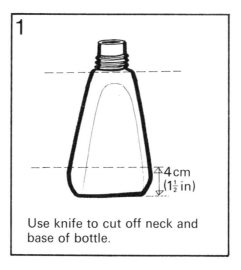

4 cm
($1\frac{1}{2}$ in)

Use knife to cut off neck and
base of bottle.

2

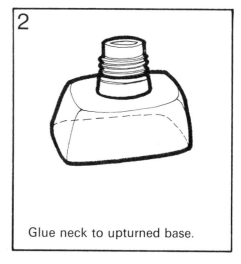

Glue neck to upturned base.

3

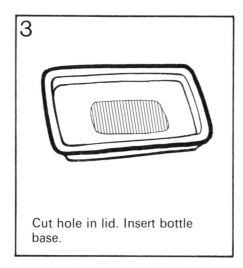

Cut hole in lid. Insert bottle
base.

4

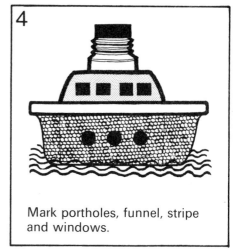

Mark portholes, funnel, stripe
and windows.

Lighthouse

**

Plastic washing up liquid bottle
Plastic cottage cheese carton or similar
Tin foil, 23 × 5 cm (9 × 2 in)
Thick paint
Black felt pen
Glue
Scissors

Quick tips:
For hint on painting plastic, see page 11.
Now add your lighthouse to a 'seascape'.
See quick tip for sailboats (page 50).

1

Cut base out of carton so that it just fits over bottle.

2

Place carton over bottle, glue if necessary.

3

Paint bottle and carton.

4

Glue tin foil around top of bottle. Mark the windows and door.

5 KING OF THE CASTLE

Cannon

**

Toilet roll tube
Kitchen towel tube cut to 15 cm (6 in)
Cheese box lid and base or 2 margarine
carton lids
2 long rubber bands
2 dead match-sticks
Thick paint
Scissors

Quick tips:
Have you made the fort (page 58) and
soldiers (page 56)?
For hints on thickening paint and painting
plastic see page 11.

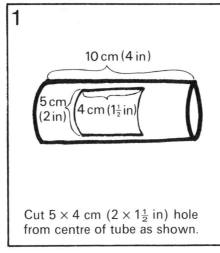

1

10 cm (4 in)

5 cm (2 in) 4 cm (1½ in)

Cut 5 × 4 cm (2 × 1½ in) hole
from centre of tube as shown.

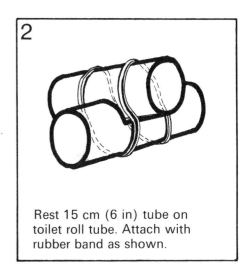

2

Rest 15 cm (6 in) tube on
toilet roll tube. Attach with
rubber band as shown.

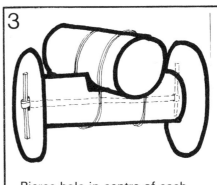

3

Pierce hole in centre of each
lid. Thread rubber band through
tube and lids, looping each end
round match. Paint cannon.

Helmet

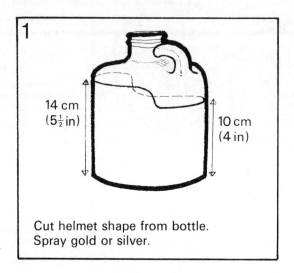

1

14 cm
($5\frac{1}{2}$ in)

10 cm
(4 in)

Cut helmet shape from bottle.
Spray gold or silver.

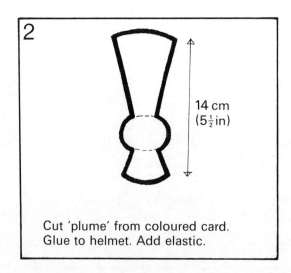

2

14 cm
($5\frac{1}{2}$ in)

Cut 'plume' from coloured card.
Glue to helmet. Add elastic.

*

$\frac{1}{2}$ gallon round plastic container (e.g. fabric softener bottle)
Piece of coloured card, 13 × 5 cm (5 × 2 in)
Spray paint, gold or silver
Glue
Elastic
Kitchen scissors

N.B. This hat is rather on the small side.

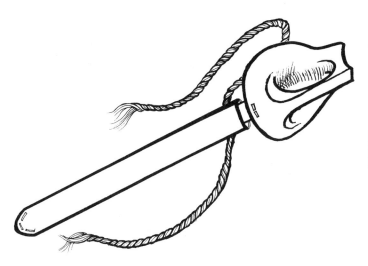

Sword and Scabbard

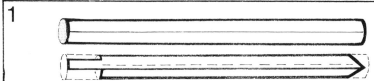

1 Cut one tube down one side. Staple together again, overlapping edges to make it flat, and slightly narrower.
Taper one end to fit handle of plastic container.
Shape the point as shown.

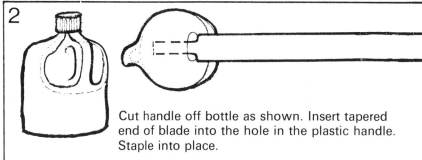

2 Cut handle off bottle as shown. Insert tapered end of blade into the hole in the plastic handle. Staple into place.

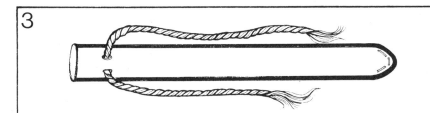

3 Flatten 2nd tube. Staple one end. Thread string through one side to tie around waist.

* *

½ gallon round plastic container (e.g. fabric softener bottle)
2 extra long cardboard tubes (e.g. tin foil tubes)
String
Stapler
Kitchen scissors

Soldier

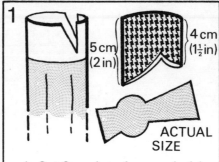

1

a) Cut 2 wedges from end of 1 tube.
b) Cut hat from other tube.
c) Cut plume from card. Glue plume to painted hat.

5cm (2in) 4cm (1½in)

ACTUAL SIZE

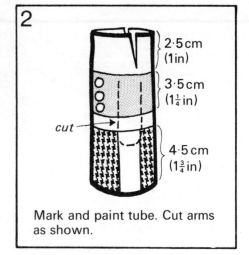

2

2·5cm (1in)
3·5cm (1¼in)
4·5cm (1¾in)

cut

Mark and paint tube. Cut arms as shown.

**

2 toilet roll tubes
Small pieces of card, black and red
Thick paint, red, blue and yellow
Glue
Black felt pen
Scissors

Quick tips:
Thicken powder paint with paste (page 11).
You could use strips of coloured sticky paper instead of paint.

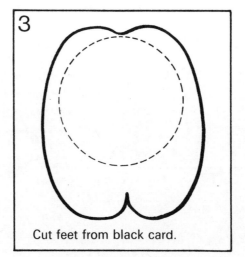

3

Cut feet from black card.

4

Mark face and hair. Push back of head inwards to close wedges so that hat will fit over it.

56

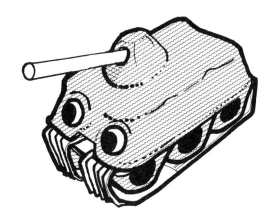

Tommy the Tank

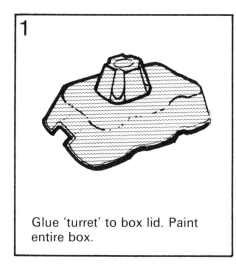

1 Glue 'turret' to box lid. Paint entire box.

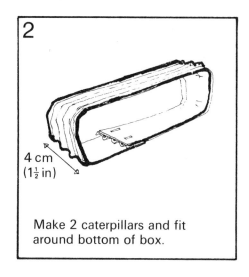

2 4 cm (1½ in)

Make 2 caterpillars and fit around bottom of box.

**

Eggbox (preferably end-opening type), plus one section
Large drinking straw, 10 cm (4 in)
Corrugated paper (e.g. from biscuit tin)
Thick green paint
Black felt pen
Glue
Stapler
Scissors

Quick tip:
Thicken powder paint with paste (page 11).

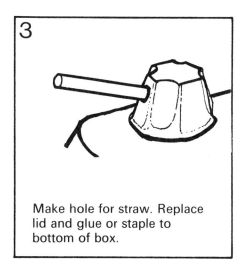

3 Make hole for straw. Replace lid and glue or staple to bottom of box.

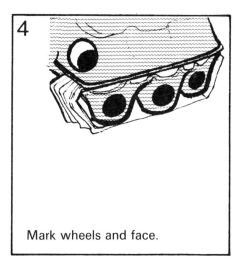

4 Mark wheels and face.

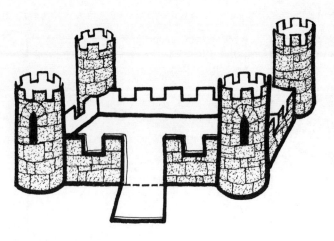

Fort

**

Large cornflakes box
4 scouring powder containers
Thick paint
Glue
Scissors
Serrated knife

Quick tips:
Add emulsion paint to water/powder paint
to help it adhere to cartons and boxes
(page 11), or scrape surface with wire wool.
Now make some soldiers (page 56).

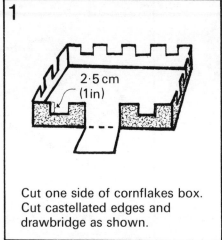

1

2·5 cm (1 in)

Cut one side of cornflakes box.
Cut castellated edges and
drawbridge as shown.

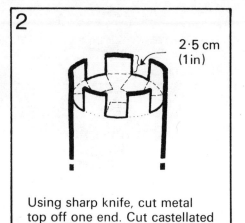

2

2·5 cm (1 in)

Using sharp knife, cut metal
top off one end. Cut castellated
edge, folding in alternate flaps.

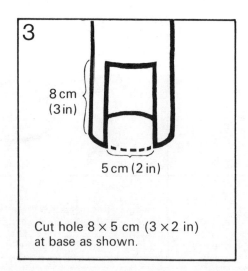

3

8 cm (3 in)

5 cm (2 in)

Cut hole 8 × 5 cm (3 × 2 in)
at base as shown.

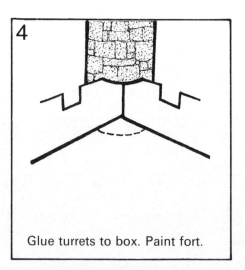

4

Glue turrets to box. Paint fort.

6 HEADS IT IS

Cowboy Hat

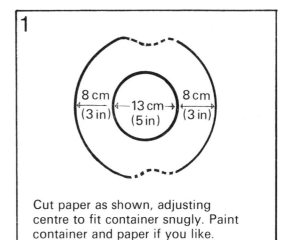

Cut paper as shown, adjusting centre to fit container snugly. Paint container and paper if you like.

*

1 lb plastic margarine carton (or similar)
Stiff paper, 30 × 30 cm (12 × 12 in)
76 cm (30 in) tape or string, cut in half
2 brass paper clips
Thick paint (optional)
Scissors

Quick tip:
For hint on painting plastic containers, see page 11.

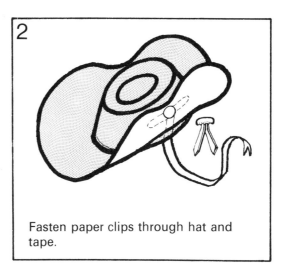

Fasten paper clips through hat and tape.

Crown

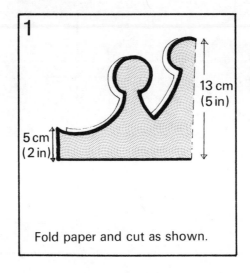

1 13 cm (5 in)

5 cm (2 in)

Fold paper and cut as shown.

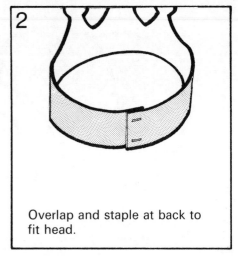

2 Overlap and staple at back to fit head.

*

Coloured stiff paper, 50 × 13 cm (20 × 5 in)
Cotton wool
Sticky paper shapes
Paste
Black felt pen
Stapler
Scissors

Quick tips:
This is just a basic crown shape. You can vary it if you like.
Pull cotton wool into small pieces and 'stretch' over pasted surface.
Design your own headband for the game you are playing, e.g. pirate, nurse, princess (tiara), indian brave, flowergirl (dried or fresh flower band).

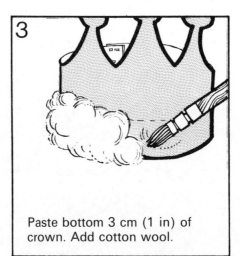

3 Paste bottom 3 cm (1 in) of crown. Add cotton wool.

4 Add sticky shape 'jewels'. Mark 'ermine' with pen.

Doily Hat, Clown's Hat and Magician's Hat

Quick tip:
You could make a princess hat by incorporating crêpe paper streamers or a piece of curtain netting into the point of the cone.

*

Doily
Circle of card, 15 cm (6 in) diameter
1 yard ribbon
Dried flowers or tissue paper
Glue
Stapler

1. Glue doily to card.
2. Glue dried flower heads all over doily to diameter of card, or use pieces of crumpled tissue paper.
3. Staple ribbon ties to card.

Quick tip:
When finished have the children parade their hats or act out the character.

*

Stiff paper, 25 × 50 cm (10 × 20 in)—
(black for magician)
Cotton wool balls for clown
Gold paper for magician
Elastic
Glue
Scissors

1. Cut half circle 25 cm (10 in) diameter out of paper.
2. Form cone to fit head. Glue seam and staple at bottom.
3. Fluff up cotton wool balls and glue to clown's hat *or* cut stars and moons from gold paper and glue to magician's hat.
4. Add strong elastic.

Ball Mask and Box Mask

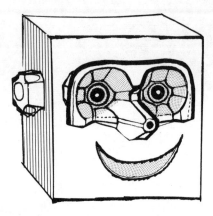

*

Coloured or painted card, 15 × 5 cm
   (6 × 2 in)
Doily
Elastic
Glue
Scissors

1. Cut out mask shape and eye holes—
   centres of holes about 6 cm (2½ in)
   apart.
2. Cut off edge of doily. Glue to back of
   mask around edge.
3. Add elastic to fit round child's head.

Quick tip:
Make a mask by drawing a face on a paper
plate.

*

Box to fit over head
Eggbox
Thick paint
Glue
Scissors

1. Use pieces of eggbox to make eyes,
   nose, ears.
2. Cut holes for eyes and mouth.
3. Paint mask.

Quick tip:
Try using a large paper bag with face drawn
on the front, but remind children never to
use plastic bags.

7 JUST FOR FUN

Goggles and Binoculars

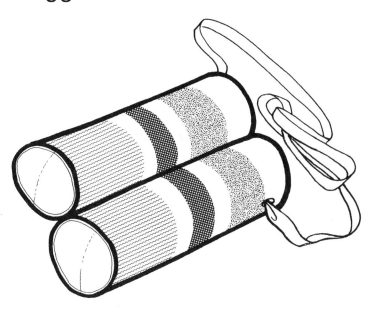

*

Eggbox (end-opening type)
Shirring elastic 30 cm (12 in)
Thick paint
Scissors

1. Cut off and trim fold-over end as shown.
2. Paint with thick paint.
3. Add shirring elastic.

Quick tips:
If you can't find this type of eggbox, try
cutting peep-holes out of two sections of
an eggbox.
Thicken powder paint with paste (page 11).

*

2 toilet roll tubes
Ribbon or string 60 cm (24 in)
Thick paint
Glue or stapler

Quick tip:
Thicken powder paint with paste (page 11).

1. Staple or glue tubes together.
2. Paint with thick paint.
3. Add strap, knotting ends inside.

*

Hen and Chick

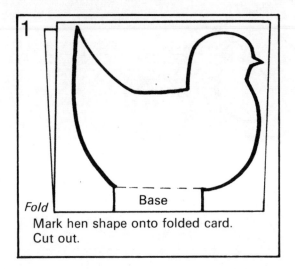

1

Fold | Base

Mark hen shape onto folded card.
Cut out.

White card or stiff paper,
   18 × 30 cm (7 × 12 in) for hen
   10 × 20 cm (4 × 8 in) for chick
Tissue paper
Cotton wool, yellow if possible
Paste
Scissors

Quick tips:
See page 92 for more ideas with tissue
paper and cotton wool.
You could make a cockerel by cutting this
shape out of bright coloured wallpaper (or
similar) and adding crêpe paper plumes for
crest and tail.

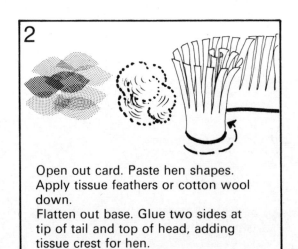

2

Open out card. Paste hen shapes.
Apply tissue feathers or cotton wool
down.
Flatten out base. Glue two sides at
tip of tail and top of head, adding
tissue crest for hen.

Monster

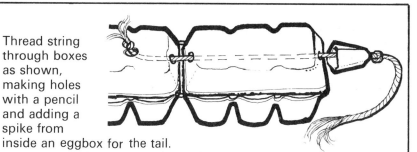

1 Thread string through boxes as shown, making holes with a pencil and adding a spike from inside an eggbox for the tail.

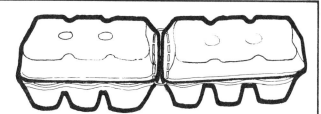

2 Link hinged ends of eggboxes with rubber band. Fix down one eggbox top with tape.

**

2 eggboxes (end-opening type)
45 cm (18 in) thick string
2 squeezy bottle tops
Large rubber band
Sticky tape
Paper, 25 × 5 cm (10 × 2 in)
Thick paint
Scissors

Quick tips:
Design your own crocodile along these lines.
Thicken powder paint with paste (page 11).

3

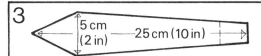

5 cm (2 in)   25 cm (10 in)

Cut tongue from paper. Fold end around elastic band. Paint monster. Make holes for eyes. Snip strip of plastic linking cap and nozzle of squeezy bottle top. Insert nozzle into eye hole, fixing cap on inside. Repeat for 2nd eye.

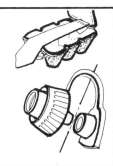

Paper Bag Puppet and Balloon

Small paper bag
Crayons or sticky shapes

1. Make face on paper bag with crayons or use sticky paper shapes.
2. Put paper bag over hand to make puppet.

Quick tips:
Use plain bags any size for making many different faces.
You could poke your fingers through the bag to make ears, nose, arms or legs.
With very small children and very large bags, you could make a paper dress by cutting holes for head and arms.

** **

Balloon
Fruit bag—net type
Small box
String
Sticky tape
Scissors

1. Cut square of net from fruit bag. Place over balloon and fix with tape at the top.
2. Attach box to net with 4 pieces of string.
3. Suspend by string from the ceiling or lampshade and put a small soft toy in the basket.

Coco the Clown

1 Cut piece of sticky paper 9 × 14 cm ($3\frac{1}{2}$ × $5\frac{1}{2}$ in). Stick around tube. Mark face, hair and arms.

2 Cut feet from card, stick on tube.

**

Toilet roll tube
Sticky paper, 15 × 15 cm (6 × 6 in)
Small piece of card or stiff paper (black if possible)
Crêpe paper
Black felt pen
Red crayon
Glue
Transparent sticky tape
Scissors

Quick tips:
You could use thick paint instead of sticky paper.
Make a tall 'clown on stilts' from a kitchen towel tube.

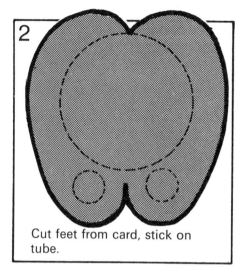

3 Cut piece of crêpe paper 2·5 × 30 cm (1 × 12 in). Snip edge. Wrap around neck and fix with tape.

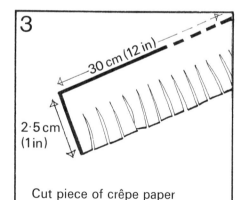

4 Cut $\frac{1}{2}$ circle 6 cm ($2\frac{1}{2}$ in) radius from sticky paper. Form cone hat to fit tube. Add cotton wool bobbles.

6 cm ($2\frac{1}{2}$ in)

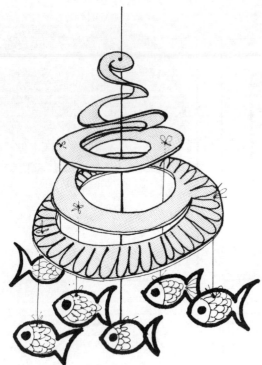

**

Paper plate
Card, 30 × 30 cm (12 × 12 in)
Thread
Scissors

Quick tips:
Use different shapes.
Use glitter or sticky paper.
Use coloured or painted card.
If mobile is lopsided, tie a piece of thread
from outer ring to the next one.

Mobile

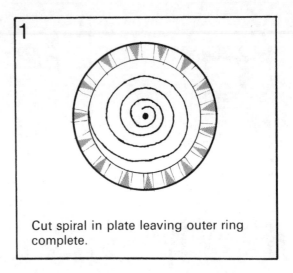

Cut spiral in plate leaving outer ring
complete.

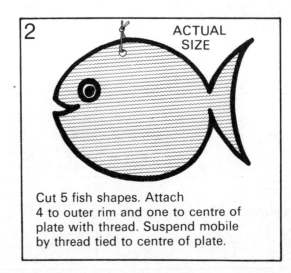

Cut 5 fish shapes. Attach
4 to outer rim and one to centre of
plate with thread. Suspend mobile
by thread tied to centre of plate.

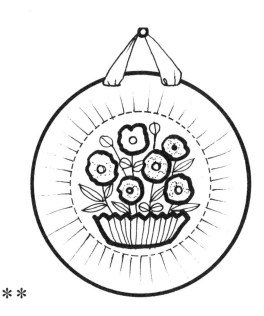

**

Paper plate
Cake case (cut in $\frac{1}{2}$)
Tissue paper (various colours)
Cord or ribbon
Crayons
Paste and brush
Scissors

Quick tip:
Chapter 10 will give you more ideas for
this type of picture.

Plate Pictures

Crayon edge of plate.
Thread ribbon
through plate.

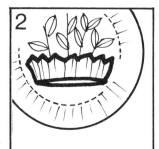

Paste edges of
cake case to plate.
Crayon leaves.

Crumple 5 cm
(2 in) circles of
tissue. Paste to plate.

* SIMPLER ALTERNATIVES

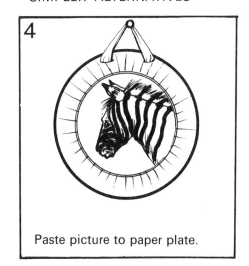

Paste picture to paper plate.

Paste picture to polystyrene
meat tray.

Weather Chart

**

2 pieces of card, 20 × 25 cm (8 × 10 in)
and 23 × 23 cm (9 × 9 in)
Brass paper clip
15 cm (6 in) ribbon or tape
Crayons or cut-out pictures and paste
Felt pen
Scissors

Quick tip:
Divide circle into eight equal segments
before adding words and pictures.

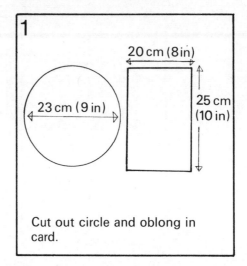

1

20 cm (8 in)

23 cm (9 in)

25 cm (10 in)

Cut out circle and oblong in card.

2

Draw pictures or use cut-out pictures. Add words.

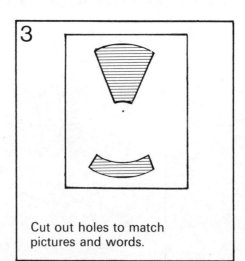

3

Cut out holes to match pictures and words.

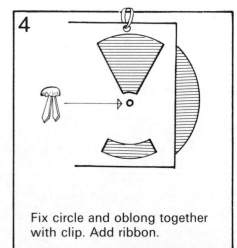

4

Fix circle and oblong together with clip. Add ribbon.

Cradles

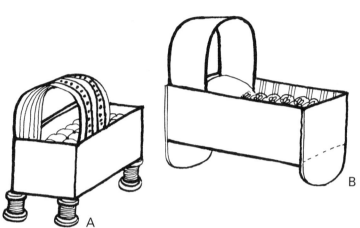

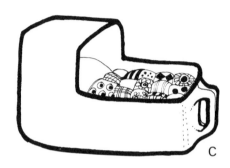

*

Shoe box
Card
4 cotton reels
Thick paint
Glue
Scissors

1.   Glue curved piece of card inside box to
     form 'head'.
2A. Glue cotton reels to base of box to
     make feet, *or*
  B. Make simple card rockers and glue to
     ends of box.
3.   Paint cradle.

*

C. $\frac{1}{2}$ gallon plastic container
    (e.g. giant washing-up liquid bottle)
Kitchen scissors

Cut corner (including nozzle)
off container.

Ballerina

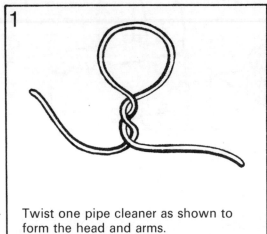

1

Twist one pipe cleaner as shown to form the head and arms.

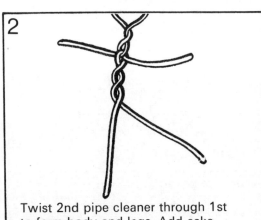

2

Twist 2nd pipe cleaner through 1st to form body and legs. Add cake case skirt.

*

2 pipe cleaners
Paper cake case

Quick tips:
You could arrange the ballerinas on a 'stage' by standing them on a polystyrene tile, or pretend they are skaters on a skating rink. Add strands of wool to make hair if you like.

Blossom Branches
and Notice Board

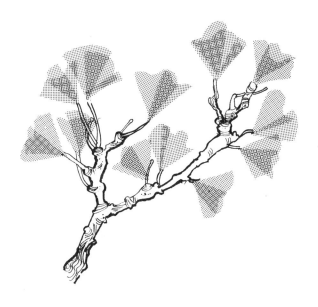

*

Branch
Tissue paper
Glue
Scissors

1. Crumple up circles of tissue paper.
2. Glue to twigs.

Quick tip:
You could use crumpled milk bottle tops
for a 'Christmas branch', adding 'snow'
from spray can.

*

Polystyrene tile, 60 × 60 cm (24 × 24 in)
Red self-adhesive carpet binding tape
Red ribbon
Red drawing pins

1. Bind edges of tile with carpet tape.
2. Add red ribbon to hang board up.
3. Pin on cut-out pictures, cards, paintings.

Quick tip:
You can make a very simple board by fixing
a polystyrene tile to the wall using a blob
of plasticine-type adhesive (page 11).

8 JUST FOR YOU

Valentine Card

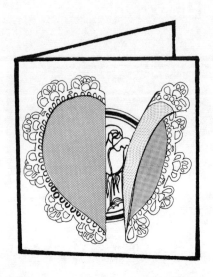

 **

Stiff white paper or card, 30 × 20 cm
  (12 × 8 in)
Stiff red paper, 15 × 15 cm (6 × 6 in)
Small doily
Picture of flower from catalogue (or crayon
  your own)
Paste
Scissors

Quick tip:
To simplify, omit doily edging.

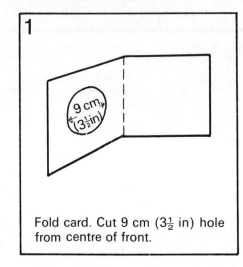

Fold card. Cut 9 cm (3½ in) hole from centre of front.

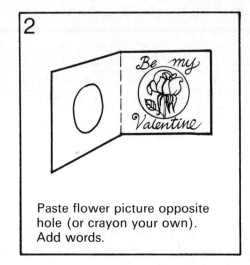

Paste flower picture opposite hole (or crayon your own). Add words.

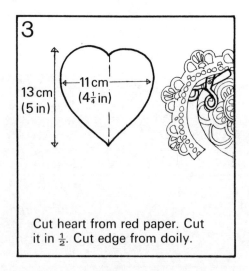

Cut heart from red paper. Cut it in ½. Cut edge from doily.

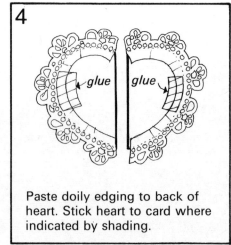

Paste doily edging to back of heart. Stick heart to card where indicated by shading.

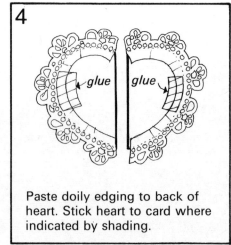

*

Tissue paper, several colours
Drinking straws
Small doily
Transparent sticky tape
Perfume
Scissors

Quick tip:
Add a ribbon if you like.

Mother's Day Posy

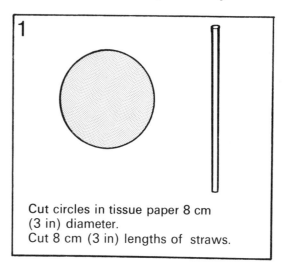

1

Cut circles in tissue paper 8 cm (3 in) diameter.
Cut 8 cm (3 in) lengths of straws.

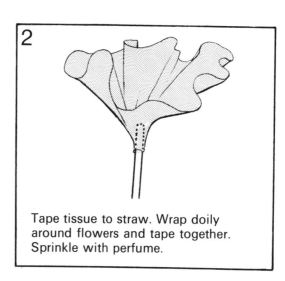

2

Tape tissue to straw. Wrap doily around flowers and tape together. Sprinkle with perfume.

Father's Day Desk-Tidy

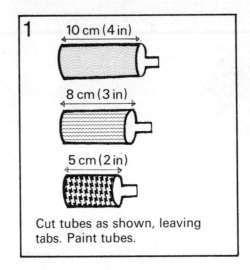

1

10 cm (4 in)

8 cm (3 in)

5 cm (2 in)

Cut tubes as shown, leaving tabs. Paint tubes.

2

Glue or staple tubes together.

**

3 toilet roll rubes
Plastic carton lid
Stiff paper or card (coloured)
Sticky paper shapes
Thick paint
Black felt pen
Glue
Stapler
Scissors

Quick tip:
You could use sheets of sticky paper instead of paper, card or paints.

3

Cut out 2 circles of paper to fit lid. Glue one in lid recess. Make slots to correspond to tube tabs.

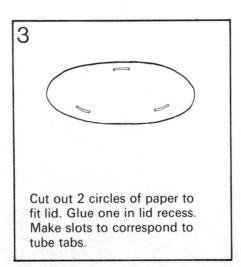

4

PENCILS

PENS

CLIPS

Place tubes on top of lid, inserting tabs through slots. Glue 2nd paper circle to base over flattened tabs. Make sticky shape lables.

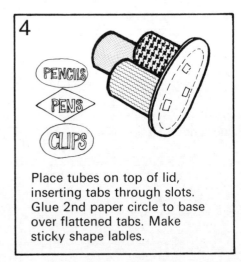

Easter Card

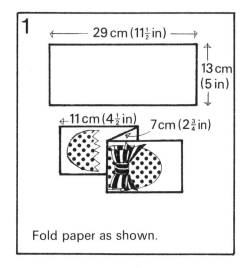

1 29 cm (11½ in) 13 cm (5 in) 11 cm (4½ in) 7 cm (2¾ in)

Fold paper as shown.

2

Draw and crayon Easter egg on outside of folded card.

**

Stiff paper, 29 × 13 cm (11½ × 5 in)
Cotton wool (yellow cotton wool ball if
    possible)
Paste
Crayons
Felt pen

Quick tip:
Simplify by crayoning chick or elaborate by decorating egg with sticky shapes or real ribbon bow.

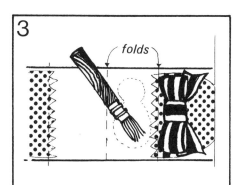

3 *folds*

Open card. Add cracked edges of shell. Mark and paste chick shape.

4 *folds*

HAPPY EASTER !

Stick small pieces of cotton wool to pasted area. Mark chick's beak, eyes and feet. Write message.

Christmas Tree

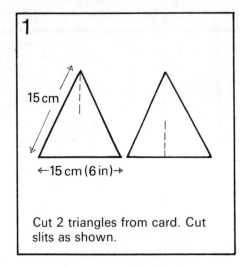

1

15 cm

←15 cm (6 in)→

Cut 2 triangles from card. Cut slits as shown.

2

Cut slots in tube as shown.

3

Fit tree together, paint green and glue to lid base.

4

Add cotton wool, tin foil stars, glitter, sticky shapes, etc.

*

Toilet Roll tube
Lid
Card
Cotton wool, glitter, sticky shapes, tin foil
Paste
Thick green paint
Scissors

Quick tip:
To make a very simple tree, slot only one triangle of card into a tube.

Cone Christmas Tree

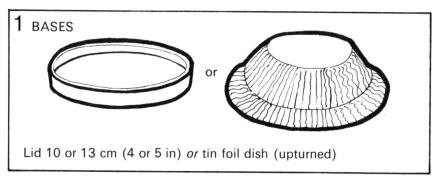

1 BASES

Lid 10 or 13 cm (4 or 5 in) *or* tin foil dish (upturned)

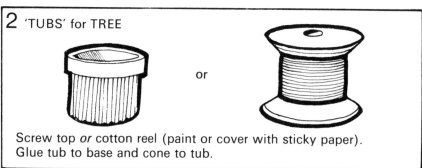

2 'TUBS' for TREE

Screw top *or* cotton reel (paint or cover with sticky paper).
Glue tub to base and cone to tub.

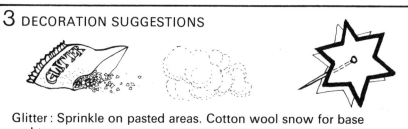

3 DECORATION SUGGESTIONS

Glitter : Sprinkle on pasted areas. Cotton wool snow for base and tree.
Star : 2 pieces of foil or sticky paper sandwiching the pin.

*

Tree: 1 large pine cone
Base: lid (cheese box or foil individual pie
   dish)
Tub: screw top or cotton reel
Decoration: glitter
              cotton wool
              tin foil and pin
Paste
Glue
Paint and sticky paper if needed
Scissors

Quick tip:
Use whichever materials are available.

Surprise Cracker

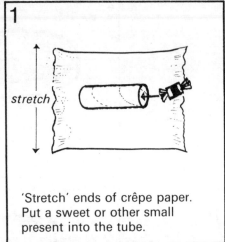

1

'Stretch' ends of crêpe paper. Put a sweet or other small present into the tube.

2

Roll crêpe paper around tube and fix each end with tape.

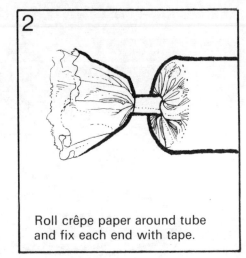

3

Spread out end of cracker as shown. Decorate with sticky stars and glitter.

*

Toilet roll tube
Crêpe paper, 15 × 23 cm (6 × 9 in)
Sticky stars
Glitter and paste
Sticky tape
Present (e.g. sweets)

Quick tip:
Decorate the cracker as you wish, e.g. paste on cotton wool snowmen, or a Christmas tree shape cut out of green paper.

*

2 doilies
2 pipe cleaners
Glue
Scissors

Quick tips:
Use coloured doilies or spray angel silver or gold.
Suspend several from a mobile (page 84).

Angel

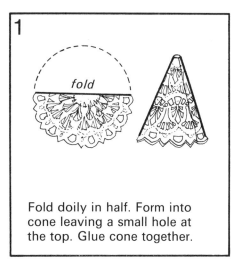

1

fold

Fold doily in half. Form into cone leaving a small hole at the top. Glue cone together.

2

Make pipe cleaner head. Insert into hole at the top of cone. Poke another pipe cleaner through cone for arms.

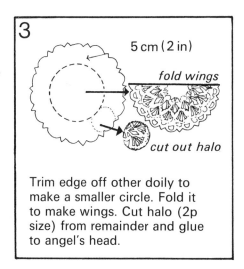

3

5 cm (2 in)

fold wings

cut out halo

Trim edge off other doily to make a smaller circle. Fold it to make wings. Cut halo (2p size) from remainder and glue to angel's head.

Father Christmas

1

Tape white paper around top of bottle. Tape red paper around the remainder. Mark arms.

2

25 cm (10 in)

8 cm (3 in)

tape

Make hat to fit head. Glue cotton wool bobble to gathered end.

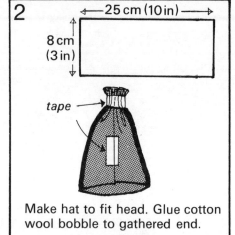

3

8 cm (3 in)

10 cm (4 in)

Cut feet out of black card. Glue to base of bottle.

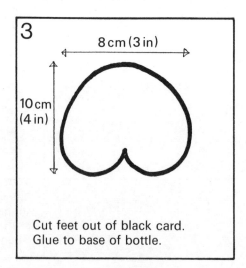

4

GLUE

Glue on cotton wool hair, beard, and trimmings to coat. Mark face.

✳✳

Plastic squeezy bottle
Cotton wool
White paper, 8 × 25 cm (3 × 10 in)
Red crêpe paper, 35 × 25 cm (14 × 10 in)
Black card, 8 × 10 cm (3 × 4 in)
Black felt pen
Transparent sticky tape
Glue

Quick tip:
'Tear' cotton wool into small pieces before gluing onto Father Christmas.

*

Scouring powder container
Toilet roll tube
Card, 15 × 10 cm (6 × 4 in)
Crêpe paper ribbon
Sticky paper shapes
Cotton wool
Thick paint
Paste
Glue
Scissors

Quick tips:
If possible, peel or scrape shiny paper
surface off scouring powder container to
help the paste adhere to it.
For simplicity, the hat could be a section of
eggbox or a large bottle top glued to card.

Snowman

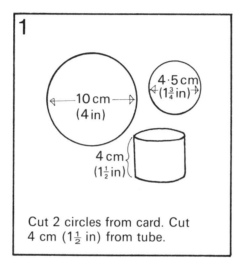

1

Cut 2 circles from card. Cut
4 cm (1½ in) from tube.

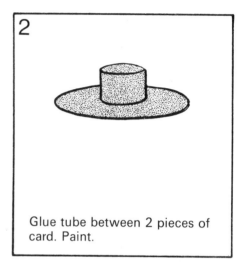

2

Glue tube between 2 pieces of
card. Paint.

3

Cover container with paste.
Stretch pieces of cotton wool
all over it.

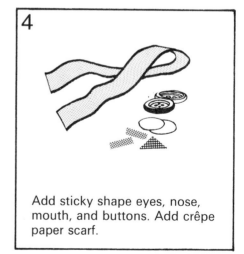

4

Add sticky shape eyes, nose,
mouth, and buttons. Add crêpe
paper scarf.

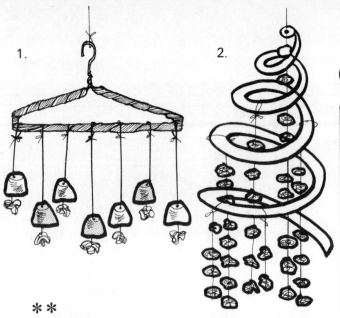

1.

2.

**

1. Wire coat hanger covered with crêpe paper
   Eggboxes
   Milk bottle tops
   Wool
   Paint
   Glue
   Glitter
   Scissors

2. Tin foil pie plate
   Milk bottle tops
   Thread
   Scissors

Quick tips:
You can use angels (page 81), butterflies
(page 20), or ballerinas (page 72) for your
mobiles.
You will find it easier to suspend the mobile
before hanging the decorations on it.

Christmas Mobiles

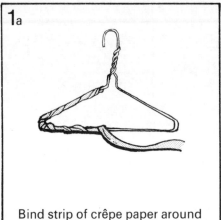

1a

Bind strip of crêpe paper around
coat hanger.

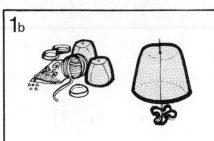

1b

Paint eggbox segments.
Decorate with glitter. Make
hole in top. Thread wool
through, knotting inside.
Crumple bottle top around
end. Tie bells to coat hanger.

2a

or
Cut spiral in foil plate

2b

Crumple bottle tops around
thread. Tie to mobile

Christmas Card and Birthday Cakes

*

Piece of folded card
Coloured sticky paper
Drinking straws
Crayons
Glue

1. Draw face on card.
2. Add sticky paper crown.
3. Glue on pieces of drinking straws for beard.
4. Write greetings inside card.

Quick tip:
You could use glitter and sequins to decorate crown.

*

Fairy cakes
Icing
Cake decorations

To celebrate birthdays, give each child a plain fairy cake, and let him decorate it with a spoonful of icing and cake decorations.

9 THE HOUSE THAT JACK BUILT
Wendy House and Castle

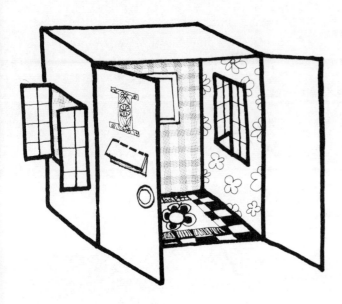

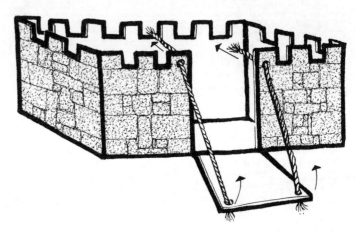

***

GROUP PROJECT
Large box (e.g., washing machine or
    television box)
Serrated kitchen knife
Thick paint

1. Cut windows and letter box.
2. Paint with thick paint.

Quick tips:
The house can be as simple or elaborate as
you like.
You could use wallpaper or paste cut-out
pictures on the walls.
Thicken paint well (see page 11).

***

GROUP PROJECT
Freezer box
Serrated kitchen knife
Thick paint
Strong cord or string

1. Cut castellated edge and
    draw-bridge in box.
2. Paint stone wall on outside.
3. Add rope supports to draw-bridge.

Post Box and Toy Box

***

GROUP PROJECT
Large box
Thick red paint
Serrated kitchen knife

1. Use knife to cut posting slot and door in
   front of the box.
2. Paint red.

Quick tip:
Make up your own postman game.

***

GROUP PROJECT
Large box
Pictures from magazine, birthday cards,
    comics, etc. . . .
Paste

Decorate box by covering with cut-out
pictures. Or you could make your own
decorations. Chapter 10 may give you some
ideas.

Bus and Boat

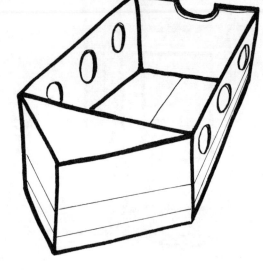

GROUP PROJECT

Large freezer box
Smaller cardboard box
Tin foil
Thick paint, red and black
Serrated kitchen knife
Glue

1. If the box is open on one side, place open side to floor.
2. Cut out windows and door-way using serrated knife.
3. Place smaller box at the front.
4. Paint bus red, wheels black.
5. Stick on tin foil for headlights.
6. You can put small chairs inside for passengers and driver.

Quick tip:
Find old or toy steering wheel and let the children dress up for the outing.

GROUP PROJECT

Large freezer box
Thick paint
Sticky tape
Serrated kitchen knife
Dinner plate

1. Draw portholes on sides of box, using the dinner plate as a pattern. Cut with knife.
2. Make bow with cardboard.
3. Cut stern as shown.
4. Paint boat.
5. Tie a broom to a chair to make a mast.

Quick tips:
Decorate a large piece of stiff paper and attach it to a pole for use as a sail.
Smaller boats can be made for one child using the same design.
To make porthole covers, do not cut complete porthole circle.

corrugated cardboard roof

HOUSE

✳ ✳ ✳

Boxes: cereal cartons etc. . . . .
Card: plain or corrugated for roofs
Thick paint
Black felt pen or black paint
Glue
Scissors

Quick tips:
For hint on painting waxed boxes see quick
tip (page 58).
You can create a whole village by painting
boxes and adding simple cardboard roofs.
The child can make his own house.

Toytown Buildings

1

FIRE STATION

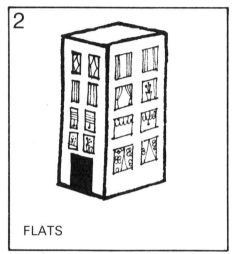

2

FLATS

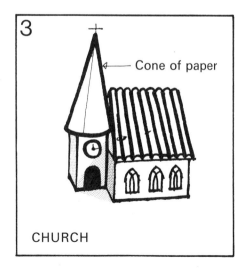

3

Cone of paper

CHURCH

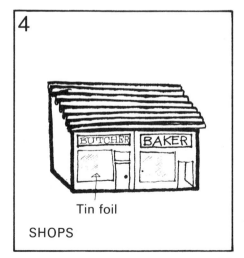

4

Tin foil

SHOPS

10 PICTURE MAKING

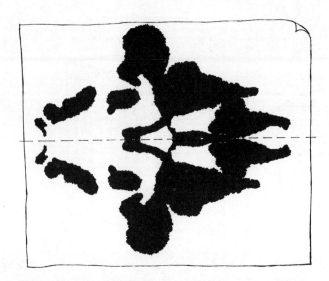

Here are some simple ideas describing various methods of making attractive pictures with or without the use of paints.

1. BLOB PAINTING

Fold a piece of paper in half. Open it up and apply blobs of paint to one side of the fold, either with a paint brush or by pouring the paint onto the paper. Refold the paper and press both sides together to transfer the pattern. Newspaper is suitable.

2. ICING SUGAR PAINTING

Mix one tablespoon icing sugar with two tablespoons water. Paint pattern with solution. Put blobs of paint on icing sugar lines. It will spread to the edge of the icing sugar but not beyond.

3. PAINTING WITHOUT BRUSHES

To make printed patterns, experiment with various objects dipped into thick paint and pressed onto paper, e.g. you could use bottle cork, cotton reel, leaves of various shapes, cotton wool, thumb, piece of corrugated cardboard or half potato. The child may be able to gouge his own pattern into a potato using a small spoon. Alternatively, use hands to spread thick paint on a smooth, washable surface (e.g. sheet of polythene). Create patterns in the paint by using hands, comb, cotton reel, string, piece of foam rubber etc. Place a sheet of paper over the paint (newspaper will do). Lift carefully to produce a print.

4. WAX PAINTING

Draw a picture with a piece of white candle. Paint over the whole sheet of paper using watery paint. The paint will not 'take' on the waxed areas. If you draw the picture first, the child can paint the paper to reveal the mystery object.

5. CUT-OUT PICTURES

Cut pictures out of magazines, shopping catalogues, seed catalogues etc., and paste to a sheet of paper to build your own picture. Here are some examples:

a) Garden—use pictures from seed catalogues to make a garden scene. You could add garden furniture, garden toys and a greenhouse. Paint a garage and garden fence if you wish.

b) House—divide a large sheet of paper into 'rooms', each about 25 × 25 cm (10 × 10 in). Paste pictures of suitable furniture, windows, appliances etc., to each room.

These could be group projects.

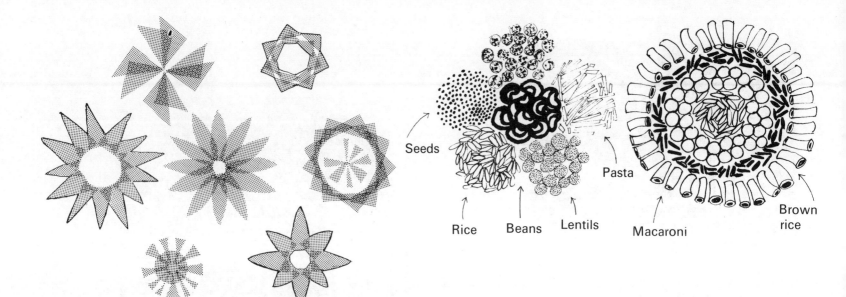

Seeds

Pasta

Rice Beans Lentils Macaroni Brown rice

6. COLOURED PAPER AND STICKY PAPER

a) Make pictures or patterns by cutting and gluing pieces of coloured paper, wallpaper, tin foil etc., to a sheet of paper. You can use bought sticky paper shapes or larger shapes cut from sticky paper sheets. A black background is effective. Try cutting out geometric shapes and arranging them into a design, e.g., train or house.

b) Use small sticky paper shapes to make a stencil design by sticking them to a piece of paper (shiny if possible so that they will peel off easily). Then crayon over entire area and peel off shapes.

7. TISSUE PAPER

This is a very versatile and colourful material. You can cut it into small pieces to make feathers, waves, fish scales, leaves etc. (cutting many layers at a time). Paste them to a white background, overlapping them slightly. Large areas can be covered in this way but always paste the background rather than the tissue paper.

Alternatively, crumple up circles of tissue paper to make flower petals, blossom on a tree or to fill in outlined shapes.

8. GRAIN AND SEEDS

Make patterns or pictures with lentils, rice, sunflower seeds, and any other dried beans, seeds and pulses that are available. Spread glue on paper, sprinkle one type of seed on it, shake off surplus. Then add other types in turn. You can make attractive flower or star patterns with circles of different seeds. A coloured background is effective.

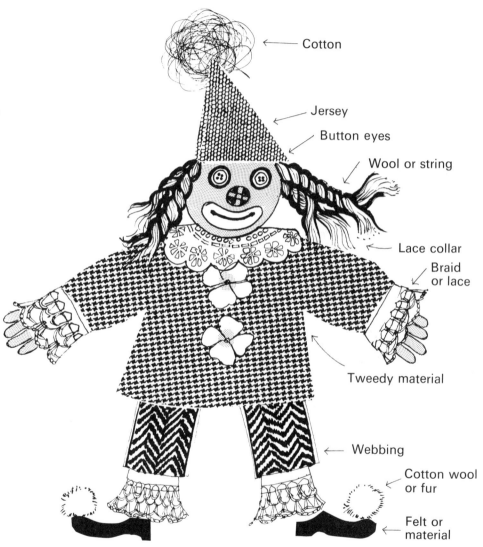

Cotton

Jersey

Button eyes

Wool or string

Lace collar

Braid
or lace

Tweedy material

Webbing

Cotton wool
or fur

Felt or
material

9. PASTA

Pasta such as macaroni or pasta shapes, can be dyed by soaking it for a few minutes in water with artificial colouring added. Dry thoroughly before using. For example, draw a house and fill in window and door shapes by gluing pasta to these areas.

Glue the paper rather than the pasta.

10. FABRIC, BRAID AND BUTTONS

Scraps of fabric, ribbon, lace etc., are widely available in many colours, patterns and textures and are very useful for collage when cut up and applied to a pasted background. The possibilities are endless and almost any subject is suitable.

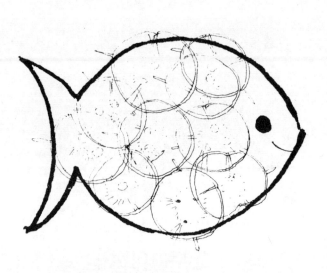
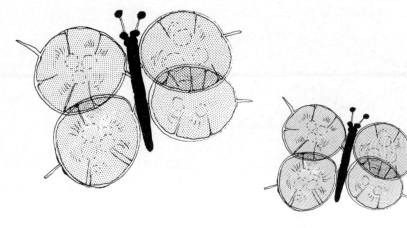

11. COTTON WOOL

Tear the cotton wool into fairly small pieces and apply to pasted areas of paper to give the effect of snow, fur, smoke or clouds.

For example, paste cotton wool to an outline of a sheep or snowman.

12. NATURAL MATERIALS

Make a picture by gluing natural materials to paper, material, felt, tin foil or cardboard.

Here are a few ideas:

Sand—for a seaside picture, put some dry sand in a tray and dip the pasted 'beach' area of the paper into the tray. Shake off surplus.
Alternatively, use golden breadcrumbs.
Shells—for the seashore or to make a snail's shell.
Sycamore 'wings'—birds in the sky.

Old man's beard—clouds.
Horse chestnut shell—a hedgehog.
Honesty pennies—butterfly wings.
Grasses, twigs, leaves, dried flowers etc.—add to a countryside scene.
Glue paper rather than materials.

To make a dried flower picture, knot a piece of ribbon through the rim of a cheese box lid. Line the box with felt and glue dried flowers to felt.
To make a shell plaque, line the inside of a plastic lid with a thick polyfilla paste (dyed with yellow paint). Press shells into polyfilla. Varnish when dry.

13. IDEAS FOR BACKGROUNDS

Paper of all colours, black and white. Tin foil on cardboard, polystyrene ceiling tiles (note that the special adhesive may be toxic), box lids, wallpaper and self-adhesive floor tiles. The latter are very useful—simply press your materials onto the tile to make a picture. Then dust the adhesive surface with talcum powder to limit stickiness.

14. FRIEZES

Several children can work together to make friezes. It is usually advisable for children to glue their finished contributions to the frieze rather than to work directly on the background. The back of a length of wallpaper makes an ideal background (tape two lengths together horizontally for extra depth).

Here are some examples, but you may think of many more subjects to follow up topics in which the children have been particularly interested.

a) Seaside—including sand for the beach (page 94), tissue paper waves for the sea (page 92), cotton wool clouds (page 94), and cut-out boat shapes.

b) Butterflies and flowers—cut out symmetrical butterfly and flower shapes. Use blob painting method (page 90) to decorate wings and petals. Paint grass and sky on frieze. Glue finished butterflies and flowers to frieze.

c) Christmas forest—cut large, simple, triangular Christmas tree shapes from corrugated cardboard (with ridges horizontal). Apply paint to one side and press onto background to make a print, but experiment on scrap paper first. Decorate trees with flattened milk bottle tops and stars. Bright green trees on a dark blue background are effective.